The Yellow Button

by Anne Mazer

illustrated by Judy Pedersen

ALFRED A. KNOPF ❧ NEW YORK

This Is a Borzoi Book Published by Alfred A. Knopf, Inc.

Text copyright © 1990 by Anne Mazer
Illustrations copyright © 1990 by Judy Pedersen
All rights reserved under International and Pan-American Copyright
Conventions. Published in the United States by Alfred A. Knopf, Inc.,
New York, and simultaneously in Canada by Random House of Canada
Limited, Toronto. Distributed by Random House, Inc., New York.
Manufactured in Singapore
Book design by Elizabeth Hardie

2   4   6   8   10   9   7   5   3   1

Library of Congress Cataloging-in-Publication Data:
Mazer, Anne. The yellow button / by Anne Mazer;
illustrated by Judy Pedersen. p. cm.
Summary: A cumulative story relating the importance
all things, large and small, hold in the universe.
ISBN 0-394-82935-2.
ISBN 0-394-92935-7 (lib. bdg.)
[1. Buttons—Fiction.] I. Pedersen, Judy, ill.
II. Title. PZ7.M47396Ye 1990
[E]—dc20   89-34921

The illustrations for this book were done in
wet and dry pastel on pastel cloth.

To my mother and father,
with love,
and
to Mr. Muffin

—Anne and Judy

Once there was a yellow button,
shiny and round,
a bit of white thread in its center.

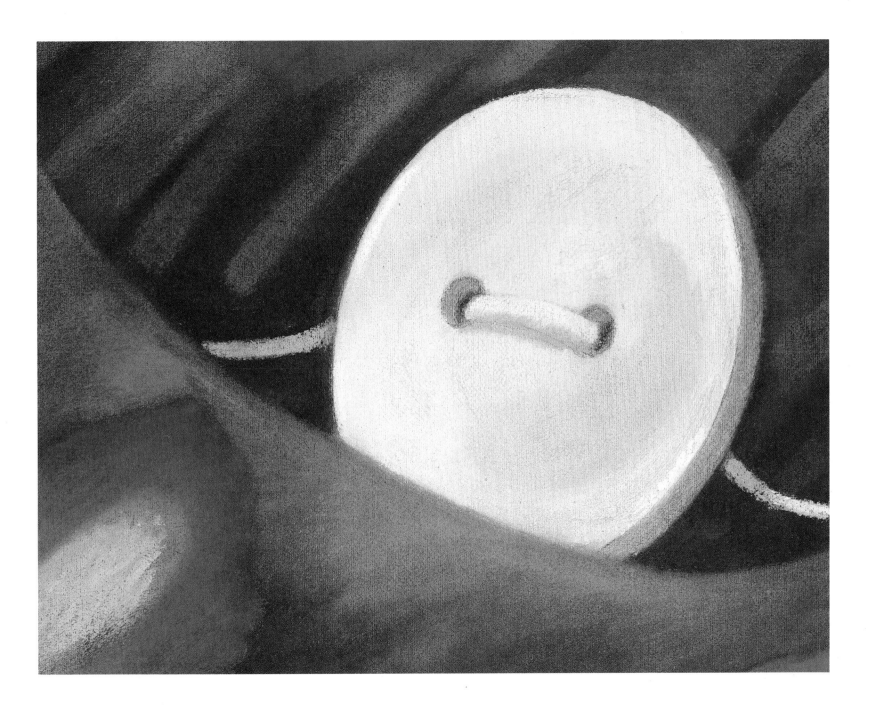

The button sat in a pocket
next to a cracker,
two pencils,
and a small key on a string.

The pocket was sewn
to a blue dress with long sleeves
and a big white sash.

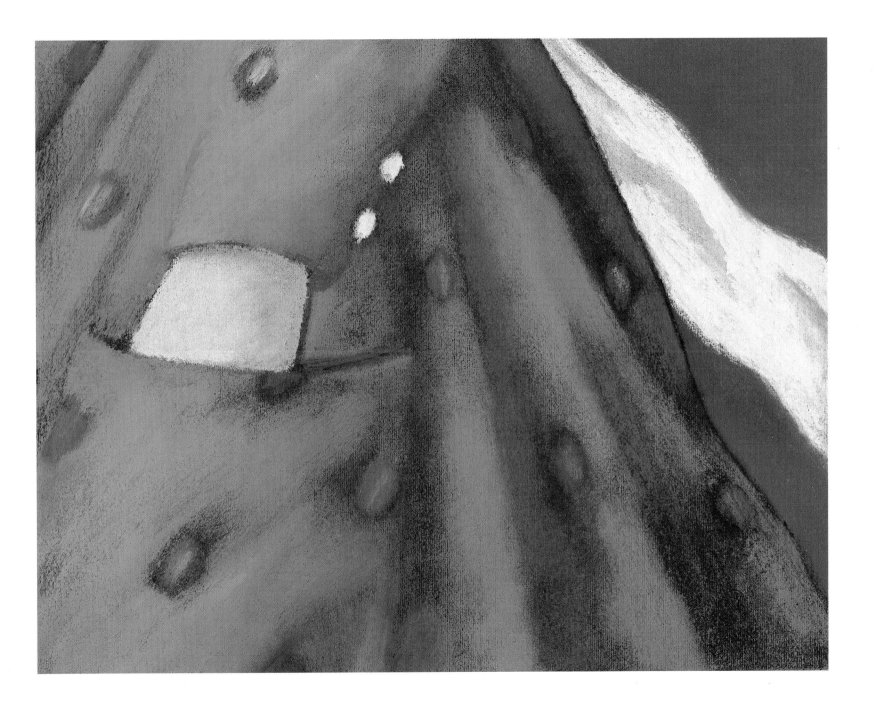

The blue dress was on a little girl
who was playing the harmonica.

The little girl was lying
near the edge of an old brown couch.

The old brown couch
was in a corner of the living room,
which was painted rose
and had pictures of the little girl
on its walls.

The living room was in a house
that was small and white
with lilacs around it.

The house was on the edge of a field
where deer grazed
and rabbits nibbled,
and where the little girl liked to run.

The field was below
a high and rocky mountain
that had pine trees and spruce
covering its slopes.

The high and rocky mountain
was part of a chain of mountains
that people climbed and hiked on
during the summer.

The chain of mountains
was in a great country
that had many lakes and forests,
fields and deserts,
cities and towns.

The great country
was surrounded by oceans,
where whales and porpoises swam
and ocean liners sailed
back and forth.

The oceans rose
and fell on the earth,
which spun round
and round the sun.
The earth was a tiny speck
in the universe, great and vast...

...and in that universe
was one yellow button,
shiny and round,
nestled in the pocket
of a little girl playing the harmonica
on an old brown couch.

Anne Mazer is the author of the recently published picture book *Watch Me*, illustrated by Stacey Schuett. She grew up in a family of writers in upstate New York, studied in France, and now lives with her husband and two small children in northeastern Pennsylvania.

Judy Pedersen made her picture-book debut with *The Tiny Patient*, which she wrote and illustrated. She was born in Brooklyn, grew up in Rhinebeck, New York, and graduated from the School of Visual Arts, where she now teaches painting. She lives in New York City.